A B
CALLED
SAUL

Fiona Cummins is an award-winning former journalist and a graduate of the Faber Academy Writing a Novel course. *Rattle,* her debut novel, received widespread praise. She has since written bestsellers *The Collector, The Neighbour, When I Was Ten, Into the Dark* and *All of Us Are Broken.* Fiona lives with her family in Essex.

Also by Fiona Cummins

Rattle
The Collector
The Neighbour
When I Was Ten
Into the Dark
All of Us Are Broken

A BOY CALLED SAUL

FIONA CUMMINS

A Quick Reads Original

PAN BOOKS

For Dad, who taught me the power of stories

1

Monday

Saul Anguish hated the police. *The filth*, his mother called them, her lip curling in disgust. Whenever a patrol car came into view, his father made pig-like grunts. 'Don't even look at them, boy.' Then he'd smack Saul on the head to remind him the Anguish family had standards.

His father was dead now and good riddance to him. His mother was an alcoholic. But their distrust of authority had seeped into their son's bones.

The boy called Saul crouched on the damp sand, inspecting it. He was not yet a man although tall enough to pass for one. Wind ruffled his hair, which was so white it seemed part of the sky. He shivered. It was a bitter day and the horizon was heavy with cloud. Even so, it was clear enough to see the small island in the distance, nestled among the salt lagoon and the trees.

Saul studied the grains of sand, darkened by seawater. He frowned, curious to understand what he was seeing. A mound of sand moved steadily in a straight line as if it were alive. He tracked it across the beach until its progress was halted by the footpath. Then a crab burrowed its way out and scuttled towards the scrubby vegetation.

He sucked in a breath. He had a good idea of its destination, an abandoned nature reserve on the island. Surrounded by mudflats and home to thousands of wildfowl, it had been reclaimed by the earth. He'd read all the newspaper stories and watched the Channel 4 programme alongside Gloria. But it had been closed to visitors for three decades.

Still, Saul had never worried much about rules.

He strode in the same direction as the crab. The air tasted of salt and seaweed. A pair of seagulls screamed at each other above his head. Fifteen minutes later, he'd crossed a narrow bridge and stood at the island's edge.

Saul had been fascinated by the natural world since he could walk. Although he had grown up in the middle of the city, he longed for something different. As a child, he'd collected dead insects in matchboxes and studied their bodies. As a teenager, his interest had grown and his heart had beaten faster with each new discovery. But it was the living population of this island that had drawn his attention today.

Saul took a step forward, listening carefully. He could hear the reedy cries of the birds. A sandpiper, perhaps? And, beyond that, a deeper sound, a sort of burrowing and scratching. He forced himself to concentrate and walked a few steps further.

A rush of movement stilled him in his tracks. Even though he had known what to expect, the sight stunned him. He wouldn't have believed it if he hadn't seen it with his own eyes.

A wall of crabs faced him, some the size of dinner plates. They were clambering over each other, too many to count. But if Saul was forced to guess, he'd have said there were at least fifty. A hundred. Probably more.

The authorities had closed the nature reserve for safety reasons after the crabs had invaded it. The crabs had arrived in ships from far-flung places and now they had taken it over, digging holes into the earth and weakening its structure. Chunks of the island's edge had collapsed into the water. It was unstable and unsafe. But Saul didn't care.

He watched them, fascinated. Their shells were dark and mottled, a muddy brown. Their claws were razor-sharp and hungry. An infestation. The stuff of nightmares.

Intrigued, he took another step closer. The crabs were focused on something he couldn't see, their movements more frenzied than he might have expected. He wondered if a deer had wandered onto the nature reserve and become trapped. Or perhaps it was an injured seabird. Even a gull with its powerful beak and wings would be no match for these invaders.

The wind had picked up. It was cold, carrying with it the promise of sleet. Saul became aware of the isolation, the creep of day towards dusk. His mobile phone was almost out of battery and there were no streetlamps until the mainland. If he was going to make it off the island before dark, he ought to leave now.

But he burned to know more.

The teenager considered what to do next. He glanced around, seeking inspiration. A large branch brought down in the previous week's gales was within easy reach. He picked it up, the bark rough against his skin. Then he poked it into the writhing mass.

They scattered immediately, a few in his direction. One grazed the surface of his trainer and he shook it off. He caught the scent of brine and rust, and a stronger smell, like rotten meat.

4

A handful of the crabs had not moved, their desire for food greater than their fear.

He could see something underneath them, but it was difficult to tell exactly what. He moved closer and the smell grew stronger. The light was fading quickly now, and Saul struggled to see. He knew he should leave but something kept him there.

One of the larger crabs began to fight with another. Their claws knocked together, making a hollow sound. Saul caught a glimpse of something pale in the sandy mulch, and the glint of gold. He crouched, aiming for a closer look, and then wished he hadn't.

It wasn't the clumps of hair that disturbed him. Or the blurred edges of what had once been flesh. It wasn't even the fingers that had been stripped to the bone.

It was the expensive gold watch. Strapped to the wrist of an arm that had once belonged to a living person. The watch's hands had stopped at twelve thirty. An idle thought popped into his head: half past noon or midnight? If Saul's suspicions were correct, he knew the answer to that.

Stealing was second nature to Saul. As a boy, he had taken trinkets from the other children. A marble here, a badge there. As a teenager, he had shoplifted meals for himself and his mother. The reward money he'd earned from saving a young child from a serial killer two years previously remained untouched, locked away in a trust. And so he scrabbled a living here and there, on the fringes of poverty.

Saul poked the crabs away again and worked quickly, unfastening the catch of the watch. One crab tried to nip him but he snatched up his hand just in time. He was not disgusted by what he was touching. It was spoiled meat, that was all. He slipped the watch into his pocket, reassured by its weight. He could get forty pounds for it at the pawn shop. Not that he planned to sell it.

It was dark by the time Saul arrived back at the flat he shared with his mother, Gloria. The dusty rooms were deserted but an empty vodka bottle sat on the kitchen table. No doubt she'd had a liquid dinner.

He checked the fridge. It contained an onion and half a block of cheese, blue mould on its rind. He could buy himself something to eat from the kebab shop. But he couldn't be bothered going out again.

With a small knife, he cut the cheese into chunks, eating around the mould. Then he placed the gold watch gently on the table, face down.

A couple of grains of sand had got stuck in the inscription on the back of the watch. Saul brushed them away with his thumb. The bulb in the kitchen had stopped working and the room was lit by the moon. In its weak light, Saul traced the name engraved on a dead man's watch.

Solomon Anguish.

His father.

2

Tuesday

Although Etta Fitzroy was no longer a detective, she still felt like one. Landing at Heathrow Airport was like coming home. Even the dingy skies and traffic clogging up the M25 motorway could not dampen her spirits.

'Could you drop me off here, please?'

The taxi driver, who had spent much of the journey talking about Arsenal Football Club, whistled. 'You a copper then?'

'No,' she said. *Yes.* Because once you were a police officer, it never left you.

New Scotland Yard, the headquarters of the Metropolitan Police. The sign outside was a little less shiny than the last time she'd been here. Probably because she was more used to New York's skyscrapers these days.

She almost hadn't come. Her old boss had called her out of the blue one afternoon. She'd been pushing Bethany in a buggy around Central

Park, watching the ducks. Her hands were cold and she'd been dreaming of a cup of tea. Not the weak American kind, but a pot of strong Yorkshire Tea.

'It's me.' She had recognized his voice immediately, if not his number. The past two years, living in America with her fiancé, Dr Dashiell Hall, and her young daughter, seemed to disappear in a heartbeat. She felt a flicker of shame and nerves. And then, excitement. These feelings confused her.

Dashiell worked at the Smithsonian, a vast museum in the city. And she took care of their child. But she missed her old colleagues and the rush of policing. And her younger sister, Nina, and nephew Max. She also missed tending Nate's grave. It had been two years since her last visit to the cemetery. She felt guilty and disloyal for abandoning the resting place of her stillborn son.

'Hello,' she had replied. Even now, she couldn't bring herself to say his name. He was The Boss. Always had been, always would be. Her breath was visible in the cold air. Life had changed since the last time they'd spoken. She'd had a child. She mentally corrected herself: *another child*.

The Boss, her former Detective Chief Inspector,

had then asked her for help on a complicated missing persons investigation. He couldn't share much more than that, but he said it was her area of expertise. He had told her that they would pay for her flights and accommodation. She would be working for the police as a freelance consultant. It would include a generous fee. It had already been signed off by the head of specialist operations.

'Since when have you had a budget as big as this?' She'd laughed as she'd said it, but The Boss had moved up in the world. He was no longer based in Lewisham in the south-east of the city. Promotion had taken him into the heart of London's policing operation. The head of the Metropolitan Police's Homicide and Serious Crime Command. He was important now. Senior. He had left her behind.

She'd been in line for promotion once. A glittering career had beckoned. She'd been sharp and bright and committed to her work. But her hot temper had let her down. That, and the faces of the murdered children she hadn't been able to save. Those cases still tormented her. Especially Grace Rodríguez, the teenager who'd disappeared on her way to a ballet exam. One of the serial killer Mr Silver's early victims. He had stripped their bones using flesh-eating beetles and displayed them in his private museum. He was dead now, a knife in his back. But his dark acts had left scars on them all. She had walked away from the police – run away, if truth be told. This knowledge made her feel small. She told herself that becoming a mother wasn't small. But she felt it. The loss of herself.

'We need help and I happen to think you're the best person for the job,' The Boss had said.

'I don't know. I can't just up and leave.'

But, it turned out, she could. Dashiell had taken one look at her face. 'You need this,' he'd said. The man who calmed her when she cried out in her sleep made some calls. His extended family would provide childcare, and he'd taken a couple of days' holiday too. And now she was here. Back in London.

The Boss's office was on the third floor. It smelled of new carpet and fresh paint. But it wasn't enough to cover up the smell of corruption. There had been many stories about abuses of power within the Met since she'd left. Racism. Homophobia. Misogyny. Etta could well believe it. But The Boss was a good man. He had high expectations, and she trusted him.

He had a few more wrinkles around the eyes these days. A few more grey hairs in his beard.

And there was a new framed photograph on his desk, a grandson. He'd once been as familiar to her as family. She reached out a hand to shake his, suddenly shy. But his face broke into a grin and he pulled her into a hug. 'I've bloody missed you. You were one of my best.'

She flushed, as pleased with his praise as she was to see him. 'Are you going to tell me what this is about?'

His expression darkened. 'I wish I knew.'

The wall of the incident room was plastered with photographs. Half a dozen women of varying ages and ethnicities. Three or four men. A couple of teenagers, their eyes sparkling with promise. In the corner, a police officer was talking quietly into a phone. But the atmosphere lacked the urgency of a live investigation.

'All of these people have disappeared in the past two years. Vanished without a trace. No activity on their mobiles or bank cards, no phone calls home. No sightings. No sign of them at all. They didn't know each other and they lived in different parts of London. None of them disappeared from the same location. They vanished at varying times of day and night.'

'What about toxicology?' It always surprised Etta how much information could be uncovered from running tests on a body. Hair, urine, blood, sweat or saliva often yielded secrets.

The Boss gave a bark of laughter. But it lacked humour. 'Chance would be a fine thing. When I said there'd been no sightings, I meant it. We don't even have a body to examine. Not a single one.'

He shook his head, as if he couldn't believe it. Then he wandered over to the window. Below them, the streets were crammed with office workers buying expensive sandwiches. It was raining. *'Life's a bitch and then you die.'* The Boss was joking, but Etta recognized the despair in his voice.

She frowned, replaying to herself what he'd said about the investigation. 'Have I understood you properly, sir? All these missing folk. They have nothing in common?'

'Correct.' The Boss winced and then dry-swallowed an indigestion tablet. Etta hid a smile. Some things never changed. 'Except for one thing.'

'Which is?'

'It's easier to show you.'

The Boss walked over to a waist-high metal filing cabinet beneath the bank of photographs. 'This is supposed to go to the evidence store, but we haven't got round to it yet.' He opened a drawer. It was stuffed with several plastic see-through evidence bags. Etta picked up the nearest one and examined it. It contained a platinum engagement ring, its diamond glinting in the artificial light. A date was etched into the ring's band.

She reached for a second bag. This time, it was a man's necklace, chunky and slightly tarnished. A pair of initials was engraved on its catch. Pure gold, judging by its weight and the typed label attached to it. Except pure gold doesn't tarnish unless there are specific circumstances.

Ting. It'd been a while since Etta had heard that bell-like noise inside her head. Some called it gut instinct, a copper's nose. But for Etta, a musical note sounded in her brain whenever a connection was made.

She sifted through more of the evidence bags. A customized Chanel keyring. A Montblanc pen. An antique silver lighter. A watch. Some of the items were clearly expensive. Others were cheaper, but still worth *something*. Each was identifiable in some way and had been traced back to its original owner.

She turned to The Boss, frowning. 'I don't understand. Where did you get these from?'

The Boss looked pained. 'That's where you come in.'

3

Tuesday

The early-afternoon sun cast its beams on the wall, highlighting a patch of grease. Dust floated in the air undisturbed. When Saul had left for the library a few hours earlier, his mother had been out. But now she was asleep, her head resting on the kitchen table. A line of drool ran down her cheek and her pink lipstick was smudged. She stank of cigarettes, cheap vodka and late nights.

For a brief time, it had seemed as if Gloria Anguish had finally pulled herself together. She'd got herself a part-time job at the Mayflower pub. The fridge was filled with meat and yoghurts, fruit and vegetables. She cooked meals for Saul. Tidied their flat. Checked that he had finished his homework. Washed and ironed his clothes.

But old habits were impossible to break. The newspaper headlines dried up. Mr Silver, the serial killer Saul had helped to catch two years previously, had faded from the nation's consciousness. As had Clara Foyle, the little girl he'd saved. The reward money landed in the trust set up for her son. Life rolled on. When the police and social services turned their gaze away from Saul, so did she.

Saul wasn't stupid. He was certain of one truth. His mother's greatest love would always be alcohol.

He sighed, his head still full of books, and filled the kettle with water. Boiled it for tea, hot and sweet and strong. Made toast with the bread he'd bought from the corner shop. Spread it with the jam he'd stolen when the shopkeeper was serving someone else.

'Is this for me?' Gloria, bird's-nest hair and sleepy eyes, smiled up at him. It wasn't, but Saul said yes, and posted some more bread into the toaster.

Gloria slurped her tea, as if she were a woman dying of thirst. 'Where have you been?'

Saul shrugged. 'Here and there.'

Gloria narrowed her eyes. She'd insisted that Saul finished school, but he didn't know why he'd bothered. He was clever, especially good at the essay subjects. But university was not for the likes of him. He didn't know what else to do with his time. He read books to keep his mind sharp, and looked after his mother. But he couldn't do that forever. He would need to get a job.

As if Gloria could read his mind, she lit a cigarette and blew out smoke. 'There are some labouring jobs going at the old Grand Hotel.'

His father had been a labourer. Hefting bricks on a development of flats along the seafront when he'd gone missing. But Solomon had also been a violent man with a sideline in drug smuggling. Saul had no desire to follow in his footsteps.

Thinking about his father reminded him of the watch he'd found the previous afternoon. It was a beautiful piece, one that he'd always wanted for himself. He eyed his mother, uncertain about whether to bring it up. Although they never spoke of it, Saul and Gloria were bonded by a violence of their own. One hot night, three years earlier, Gloria had killed her abusive husband. Under intense pressure, Saul had disposed of his father's body in the sea. It was a miracle, really, that his watch had survived. But the tide always returned its treasures in the end.

Luckily for them both, saltwater and the passage of time had made Solomon Anguish unrecognizable.

He didn't answer her, but busied himself with

washing up their plates. She was droning on about a man she'd met in the pub. He was coming back tonight, apparently. Not for the first time, Saul thought she sounded like a radio playing in the background. He wished he could turn her off. His eyes drifted around the kitchen. The pile of unopened mail. The dried bird's mess on the pane of glass. The empty windowsill.

Saul's gaze returned straight back to the windowsill. Still empty. But he'd left his father's watch there, drying overnight on a piece of kitchen roll.

He turned to his mother, interrupting her monologue. 'Did you take the watch? The one on the windowsill?'

'No. I haven't seen a watch.' But Gloria's eyes slid away from his, and he knew she was lying.

'Where is it?'

'I don't know what you're talking about.' She stood up and he glimpsed a necklace of bruises marking her skin. Briefly, he wondered if she was having sex with violent strangers again. 'But you need to be more careful with your things.'

Her attitude made him angry. She had no idea what she'd taken. Or perhaps she had. Either way, Saul was sure this would bring trouble to their door.

A part of him wanted to shake the truth from

her. To give in to the anger that ran through him with a fierce intensity. He took a step towards her. He was taller than she was. Taller than his father had been. He could squeeze the truth from her, his hands around her neck. Beat it from her like his father might have done. For several seconds, Saul fought with his temper and his conscience.

But he was saved from himself by an insistent knock at the front door.

4

Tuesday

The once-upon-a-time detective Etta Fitzroy followed The Boss back to his office. He indicated that she sit down. Then he placed an evidence bag on the desk in front of her. It contained a yellow-gold watch.

'Remember our old friend Mr Silver?'

How could she forget? A serial killer with multiple aliases. Brian Howley. The Night Man. Ol' Bloody Bones. The Collector.

'Yes.' She was wary. He still haunted her in nightmares.

'Don't worry, he's long gone, but do you remember that boy? The teenager with the blond hair and the alcoholic mother?'

No one who had met him could forget Saul Anguish. A boy touched by darkness. Groomed by Mr Silver. A childhood of neglect. A hero? Definitely. Saul's actions had saved five-year-old Clara Foyle and netted him a big reward.

A killer? Probably. She'd always suspected it was Saul who'd stabbed Mr Silver during that final showdown. But the case had never gone to trial. 'Of course. Why?'

'This watch belonged to Saul's father. Solomon Anguish has been missing for three years.'

She remembered. The Boss had always suspected there was something suspicious about his sudden disappearance. And so had she.

'Where did you get it from?'

'Turned up at a pawn shop this morning. Sold by none other than Gloria Anguish for thirty-five pounds.'

Etta furrowed her brow, confused. 'I don't see the connection. Perhaps she needed money. Isn't it likely she was going through her husband's belongings for items to sell?'

The Boss shook his head. 'It's possible, I suppose. But we don't think that's the case here. The watch showed traces of saltwater damage. Try again.'

Etta thought through everything she knew so far. The Boss had summoned her from the States before the watch turned up. But it was clearly relevant in some way to his line of questioning. A thought occurred to her. 'Wait, did the other items you showed me turn up at the same pawn shop?'

21

'Bingo.' The Boss grinned. 'Some of them had also been damaged by saltwater. What else?'

She concentrated for a minute, listening for the music in her mind. Being out of the police might have left her a bit rusty. But she had an instinct for patterns. For solving puzzles.

She spoke slowly, trying to work it out as she went. 'Gloria sold all the other items too?'

'Correct. Gloria, and sometimes Saul.' The Boss's face broke into a wide grin. 'I knew you'd get it.'

'How do you know this?'

'One of the missing women is the wife of a jeweller. She was wearing her engagement ring when she disappeared. It was bespoke and distinctive, designed especially for her. We'd circulated photographs of it when she first disappeared. When it turned up recently, the pawnbroker tipped us off. We checked what else Saul and Gloria had sold over the past few months. Bits and pieces here and there. Probably picked up from car boot sales or possibly stolen. But we also noticed that several of the items were connected to those reported missing.'

He paused for breath, his face creasing in concentration. 'We asked the pawnbroker to call us as soon as they tried to sell anything else. We sent someone to collect the watch this morning.'

'OK, so where do I come in?'

The Boss leaned forwards, his face grave. 'We decided to wait for you to arrive before we tried to talk to the Anguish family. You had a rapport with Saul, remember? If he's going to open up to anyone, it would be you.' This morning's discovery of his father's watch only made this request more pressing.

But Etta was unconvinced. There was a wolfish wariness to the boy that had unsettled her, even then. She had felt sympathy for him. A desire to help. But his hardness made him difficult to reach.

'I don't know.' She was not sure if she wanted to revisit this part of her life. Some nights, she woke up screaming, tormented by those she had failed to save.

But then she thought of her daughter Bethany, loved and cherished by her family. Safe and warm at home. Food in her tummy. A mother and father who would give up their own lives to protect hers. Perhaps she could help Saul. If a boy like him wanted her help.

Her mind drifted. She wondered what to do with her luggage. She was reminded of the night Clara Foyle had disappeared. She hadn't thought about it for years. Etta, then a detective sergeant, had turned up at the Foyle family's house,

23

dragging a suitcase behind her, a night in a hotel cut short. It was another time from another life. But Saul Anguish had been part of that story too. She hoped this symmetry wasn't a bad omen.

She gave a terse nod. The Boss, who had been watching her closely, grinned again. 'I was hoping you'd agree. Leave your suitcase here. We'll get it sent on to your hotel.'

'Am I going on my own?' She didn't want to say it out loud, but she felt nervous. Unprepared for the challenge.

'I thought you might like some company. Detective Sergeant Antonia Storm is waiting for you in a car downstairs.'

5

Tuesday

Saul looked at Gloria. Gloria looked at Saul. Both of them knew that an unexpected knock on the door was never a good sign.

Gloria grabbed her fake-fur leopard-print coat and disappeared out of the back door. Saul knew she would cut across the gardens and down the side alleyway. He cursed to himself. It was typical of his mother to leave him alone to deal with this.

He could ignore it. But something told him that whatever 'it' was, it wasn't going away. From the top of the stairs, he had a perfect view of the front door. Through its opaque glass window, he could make out two heads. His stomach dropped. Two heads meant one of three things. 1) The authorities – social services, the council or the police. 2) The church, probably Jehovah's Witnesses. 3) Thugs who intended to do harm.

He slid on the chain and opened the door a fraction. Two women stood on the doorstep.

They were dressed too smartly to be from social services. Neither was carrying a religious leaflet. One of them had a pair of handcuffs hanging from her utility belt. His hackles rose. Police, then.

'What do you want?'

The one with a mass of brown curls and tired eyes spoke first. 'Hello, Saul. Remember me?'

He stared at her. Did he? She seemed vaguely familiar. Like an old school teacher. Or the mother of one of his mates. He sneaked another look. She had different-coloured eyes. One blue. One brown.

'Do we know each other?'

'We did. I was there in the Crooked House on the night Mr Silver died.'

Saul's eyes widened. He never allowed himself to think of that night. It was packed up and parcelled away. But the sight of Etta Fitzroy brought the memories rushing towards him.

'How's Clara?'

'Doing well, I think. I left the police soon afterwards, but now I'm back for a bit.'

'Why are you here?'

'If you let us in, I'll explain.'

For the second time that day, a reluctant Saul made tea for someone else. The spare mugs were chipped. The milk was going off. A sense of shame consumed him, and it made him defensive.

'We don't have any biscuits.'

'We don't mind, do we, Toni?'

DS Antonia Storm patted her stomach. 'I've already had an apple pie and a Crunchie today. I definitely don't need biscuits.'

Saul stood awkwardly in the corner of the living room. The women sat side by side on the lumpy sofa. He saw the room through the eyes of strangers. An old rug, threadbare in places. Gloria's sewing machine, gathering dust. A TV with a crack in its screen after his mother had thrown a shoe at it. But their gaze was drawn to the large window that looked out upon the estuary. Even though Saul was used to it, the view was breathtaking.

A flock of seagulls stood out against the clouds. The vast sky was streaked with the colours of a late autumn afternoon. Gunmetal grey. A hint of blue and silver. The sense that night was not too far away. The tide was out, revealing a thick layer of mud that smelled of seaweed and salt. But it would not be long before the fishing boats were bobbing on the water again. The push and pull of the tidal flow was as natural as breathing.

Etta took a sip of her tea. If she noticed the lumps of sour milk floating on its surface, she didn't comment. 'How have you been, Saul? You and your mother?'

He had never liked questions. Especially not ones from the police.

'Fine.' The women shared a glance. He knew what it meant. He was difficult. Hard work. People had used these words to describe Saul for as long as he could remember. Especially those in authority. 'Why are you here?' he said again.

Etta's reply electrified him. 'Where did you find your father's watch?'

He forced himself to breathe slowly. To remain calm. She could not possibly know the answer to that. *What the fuck have you done, Gloria?* 'Where do you reckon?' It was the best answer he could think of under pressure. If he sounded rude, he didn't care.

'I don't know. That's why I'm asking you.' She paused, her voice softer. 'You're not in trouble. Neither's your mum. But it could be important to an ongoing investigation.'

His face was pale and pinched. He didn't want to tell her. Because if he told her, she would ask him to take her there. And if they found his father's remains, it would lead them back to his mother. To him. Did DNA survive in saltwater? What about forensic evidence? Saul didn't know. He didn't *think* so. But he couldn't be sure.

So he said nothing, hoping she would let something relevant slip.

'Did you know your mother sold your father's watch this morning?'

Stupid, stupid bitch. 'It wouldn't surprise me,' he said carefully.

'To a pawn shop in town.'

He nodded, watching both women. Waiting to see what would happen next.

'Do you sell things there, too?'

He knew then that they had him. Perhaps this wasn't about his father's watch at all. He cursed his own stupidity. His mother's greed and thirst for alcohol. One bottle was never enough for Gloria fucking Anguish. Of course it wasn't. And it was so expensive to buy these days. Much harder to steal with security tags on the bottles. Her addiction drove them to pawn things that didn't even belong to them.

There were CCTV cameras all over that pawn shop. The shopkeeper kept a careful log of all goods bought and sold. He had shafted Saul and Gloria at the first opportunity. And who could blame him?

'Sometimes.' Saul was cautious. Reluctant to say too much. Did he need a lawyer or something? He wasn't sure he'd broken any laws. As far as he knew, he didn't have to report a dead body to the authorities. Not one he'd accidentally found. It was a quirk of the law. He had learned that during his A-level sociology lessons at school. *Stay calm, Saul. Stay focused and alert*, he thought to himself.

'Where did you get them from?' asked DS Storm. 'Those items you pawned.' She opened her notebook. The sight of it made him nervous. His hands felt clammy and a muscle pulsed in his thigh. He wanted to run. To race across the beach, away from their stupid questions and their serious faces. To stand on the edge of the cliff and shout into the wind. Etta shot him a warning look. He didn't know what it meant, but he decided then to tell the truth.

'I found them.'

Etta frowned. 'That's not possible, Saul.'

'It is.' He was insistent. 'I can show you now, if you want. But you might need a torch.'

6

Tuesday

Etta was so exhausted she could barely keep her eyes open. She had flown 3,500 miles from New York to London. She had gone straight from Heathrow Airport into a meeting with The Boss. And now here she was on the Essex coast, jet-lag dragging her towards sleep.

It had been a wonderful surprise to see Toni Storm again. She was still as elegant and well groomed as she'd always been. The women had started out as fierce rivals and ended up as close colleagues. Etta had made a mistake once that had almost cost Toni her life. Almost, but not quite. A friendship had blossomed from a shared sense of humour and a liking for breaking the rules. Their friendship had survived motherhood, and promotion, and Etta's move to New York.

As for Saul, the past two years had changed him. His boyishness had all but vanished. He was eighteen now, technically an adult, but still wore the traces of his neglected childhood. His face had hollowed out, lending him a hunted look. He was scared of something. Or someone. But she was too cold and too tired to give it much thought.

They should have said no. She should have insisted on coming back tomorrow morning. But DS Storm was like a dog with a bone. If she thought she was onto something, she wasn't letting go.

It had begun to rain. With a sinking heart, she remembered her waterproof coat was still in her suitcase. Her stomach rumbled. She couldn't remember when she'd last eaten. Probably on the plane. A wave of homesickness hit her. She missed Bethany and Dashiell with every part of herself.

The three of them trudged along the cliff path in the encroaching darkness. The last time Etta had been here was during the hunt for little Clara Foyle. Shouted voices and torches. The discovery of a rabbit skeleton, Mr Silver's calling card. She felt panicked, afraid. A drum-beat in her heart and her head. Post-traumatic stress disorder. Even though they'd caught the killer. Even though the monster had been slain.

Saul led them down the cliff steps, slippery in the weather. A part of her wondered if they should trust him. It was difficult to talk against the noise of the wind and the incoming tide. She pressed a hand into Toni's side, a warning of sorts. Toni squeezed it. She understood.

By the time they reached the bridge that led to the island, Etta was soaked through. Rain dripped from the ends of her dark curls and down her back. Her leather shoes were ruined. A metal sign was rusted around its edges. Toni held up her torch. DANGER! CLOSED TO THE PUBLIC.

'Wait,' said Toni. 'I know this place. It's been out of bounds for years.' She turned to Saul. 'It's not safe, especially in the dark.'

Saul shrugged, but his expression was cold. Etta read the challenge in it. He was testing them. She nudged Toni again. 'We're here now. We might as well take a look.'

Toni sighed. 'Same old Etta. But if I think it's too dangerous, we'll come back at first light.'

The island was covered in dense vegetation. At times, it was impossible to tell where the path should be. Rain dripped continuously from the leaves, shiny in the torch-light. The place was alive with something they could hear, but not see. Etta sensed movement, but it was too dark to be sure. The ground was a mixture of sand and earth. It smelled of something dank and rotten. Something unholy.

Saul guided the women to the northern edge of the reserve. There was an inlet here that crossed the hump of the island. It was here the incoming tide delivered its treasures. Empty bottles. The matted remains of fallen seabirds. The occasional rat. Rotting fish. Random bits of clothing. Discarded rubbish. And dead bodies.

'Here,' said Saul. 'This is where I find them.'

At first, neither woman understood what he meant. But then Toni swept her torch in the direction that Saul was pointing in.

A crab scuttled out of the undergrowth, the size of a dinner plate. Quickly followed by another. And another. Toni screamed. Etta sucked in a sharp breath. Saul laughed at them both. He seemed to get a kick from their fear.

'They won't hurt you.'

'What are they?' Etta's voice was steady in the darkness.

'Chinese mitten crabs. Massive, aren't they?' He waved his arm towards the scavengers, which had arrived in the UK decades earlier. With their fur-covered claws, they'd gained a reputation for eroding habitats and destroying native species. 'They've taken over the island. There's hundreds of them.' He turned to Toni, finally relenting. 'You'll need to lower your torch.'

Toni didn't answer him. But her torch swept

back and forth across the ground. Methodical. Determined. The beam of light criss-crossed a mound of rocks. A tattered fishing net. A collection of spiky seagrasses. Until at last she found what she was looking for.

'Dear God,' she said. Etta stood next to her. Both women bowed their heads. Even Saul had the sense to stay quiet. This place was a graveyard of human remains. Of lost souls. Neither woman needed a forensic pathologist to confirm what they could see with their own eyes.

Piles of bones, hundreds of them. Bodies in varying states of decomposition. Etta recalled her training from the police college at Hendon. Cold water slowed the rate at which a body rotted. Some could last in the depths for several weeks. A skeleton was still recognizable after five years.

She placed the cuff of her sweater across her mouth. The scent of death was stronger here. It was laced with the distinctive mud of the Thames Estuary. And the marine life that inhabited it.

'Where did you find your father?' Her voice was gentle.

Saul pointed to a pile of bones that had once been Solomon Anguish. They were still in the same place he'd found them. By a quirk of fate, the tide had brought him ashore, flesh still clinging to his remains. But the crabs had stripped him clean overnight. If the sea lice and fish had nibbled at him, the crabs had finished the job.

'I'm sorry,' she said. The boy's face was pale in the moonlight. He was expressionless. She couldn't decide if it was shock or disinterest. 'Does your mother know?'

Saul shook his head. 'I didn't tell her.'

Etta wondered how Solomon Anguish had ended up here. Drunk? Murdered? Perhaps he had killed himself, walking into the sea with rocks in his pockets. Or had he simply lost his way in the dark? It was possible they would never know. She kept those thoughts to herself for now.

Toni was fumbling at her belt for her handset. 'I need to call this in.'

Two hours later, the small nature reserve on the Essex coast was cordoned off. Blue and white police tape fluttered in the wind. Several lamps had been erected. Their white light illuminated the wet leaves and the dullness of the bones. The crabs kept their distance, preferring shadows to the brightness and activity.

The Boss rang Etta. 'Bloody hell. You've been here two minutes and you've made more progress than we've done in the past few months.'

'Beginner's luck.' She laughed. It felt good to be back. There was still a case to be cracked. How the bodies had turned up here and why. But, for now, they had a promising new lead. And answers, however tragic, for several families.

She yawned, her jaw cracking. They were all wet and tired. Bed beckoned. 'Come on, Saul. Let's give you a lift home.'

7

Tuesday

Saul could tell as soon as he entered the flat that it was empty. He showered and dressed in his warmest clothes. Then heated up a pizza and ate it in neat mouthfuls, sitting in the dark.

He wasn't sure if he'd done the right thing, revealing those bodies to the police. He'd never intended to take anyone to what he thought of as *his* island. But he didn't feel like tying himself up in knots with their enquiries. *Ask me no questions, I'll tell you no lies.* And he hadn't. He'd told them the truth, just not about his father. As long as Gloria held her nerve, they'd be fine. Although, with the island now out of bounds, they'd need to find new ways to make money.

He typed out a message to his mother: WHERE ARE YOU?

When she was drunk, she was unpredictable. He needed to be sure she could stick to their

38

story. But first, they needed to decide what that story was.

He waited until midnight for her to reply. He waited until the moon was at its peak, its reflection rippling on the surface of the water. He waited until he could physically wait no longer. Then his eyes closed and he fell into a fitful sleep on the sofa. Still waiting for the sound of her key in the lock. Still caring for his mother, even though she was incapable of caring for him.

Something woke him up. The tip of his nose was cold. He blinked into the darkness. His arm felt heavy, that pricking sensation of pins and needles. In the distance, an owl screamed as it hunted rats on the cliffs. His ears caught the scuffle of some animal. A pair of foxes scrapping over their territory. Perhaps a badger. It was late, or early. He checked the clock on his phone. 4.24 a.m. And still no word from his mother.

He headed into the kitchen, to check if she'd been there. But it was exactly as he'd left it, his plate drying next to the chipped mugs. No vodka bottle or wine glass. No mug with its imprint of lipstick. No shoes kicked off carelessly for him to trip over. No leopard-print fake fur hanging on the coat peg. An absence of cigarette smoke. An absence of Gloria.

It wasn't the first time Gloria hadn't come home and it wouldn't be the last. Saul rubbed his eyes and then stumbled into his bedroom. He fell asleep almost immediately.

When he woke up again, it was mid-morning, a blade of light through his curtains. He stretched, unused to such a lengthy sleep, then realized he was shivering. The temperature had dropped again and the boiler was broken. He reached for his coat, but it was still damp from the previous night. He wrapped his duvet around his shoulders.

'Gloria.' Her name echoed around the empty flat when he called out for her. But she did not reply. He made tea to warm himself up.

At the kitchen table, he checked the credit on his phone. Almost gone. He rang her, but it went immediately to her voicemail. He didn't leave a message.

On the back of an envelope, Saul made a note of his mother's friends. A list of her favourite pubs, and her workplace. He wrote the word hospital in capital letters and underlined it. There was a sick feeling in the pit of his stomach. He remembered the time she had nearly drowned and how Mr Silver had saved her life.

He did not want to call the police. He'd had

enough of them in the past few hours. And they wouldn't care about a woman like Gloria. It was Wednesday now. Today was her birthday, and she had promised to buy him fish and chips for tea. Even though she didn't always keep her promises. Even though she had probably spent the money on drink. He had bought her a necklace, a silver shell. He had paid for it by doing a few odd jobs for the old man next door.

If she still wasn't home by dinnertime, he'd start looking for her.

8

Wednesday

'It's to do with tidal flow.' The police officer from the Marine Policing Unit pushed his spectacles back up his nose. 'Most bodies that fall into the Thames in London get stuck in the U-bend.' At their blank looks, he explained further. 'The curve of river around the Isle of Dogs.' He shook his head at the grim image that conjured. 'Most. But not all of them.'

DS Toni Storm was making detailed notes, her pen moving across the paper at speed. But Etta was watching the river. It was as relentless as time, never still, always moving forward. It took two minutes for the shock of cold water to paralyse limbs. To sink. Then drown. At least, that's what PC Tim Chandler had told them.

Two minutes to live or die.

They were standing outside an unremarkable building on the north bank of the Thames at Wapping. At the headquarters of the MPU, also

42

known as the river police. Tower Bridge, Etta's favourite bridge, loomed in the distance.

'So it's unlikely the bodies entered the water here in London?' Toni tapped her pen against her bottom lip.

PC Chandler raised his eyebrows. Several fine lines appeared on his forehead. 'It's difficult to say for sure. Only the river knows where and when a body will resurface.'

Within minutes of being in PC Chandler's company, Etta had discovered several facts about the River Thames. Two stood out. The river police discovered more bodies they couldn't identify than those they could. And a corpse was retrieved from its 213-mile stretch roughly once a week.

'The mouth of the Thames is at Southend-on-Sea. Not far from where your bodies were found. It's possible they were dragged onto the island by the tidal flow towards the North Sea.'

'But you can't tell us where they might have gone in?'

PC Chandler laughed, showing off his teeth. 'That's like trying to find a needle in a haystack.'

Etta and Toni walked back towards central London via the Thames Path. Etta counted off their missing persons on her fingers. 'Two were homeless. One was a sex worker. Three had mentioned feeling suicidal. At least two had ongoing issues with alcohol. One was Saul's father. Is it possible they all entered the Thames at different points—?'

'—but ended up in the same place?' Toni finished her sentence. 'So coincidence?'

'Not coincidence,' said Etta. She mimicked pushing glasses up her nose, like PC Chandler. '*Tidal flow.*'

'It's possible,' said Toni. 'Probable? I don't know.'

The Thames Path was busy for a Wednesday morning. Cyclists. Joggers. Babies being pushed in prams. Businesspeople in suits, walking briskly in the autumn chill. Below them, the river continued its unstoppable flow.

'What if we haven't been able to find a connection between the missing people because there isn't one?' Etta watched a police boat race by at speed. She wondered which unfortunate soul they were looking for. And whether they'd be in time.

'Not a serial killer then?' Toni's tone was flippant, but both women knew it hid a darker fear. Toni had almost died after breathing in poison during a raid on Mr Silver's house.

But Etta didn't know the answer to that.

*

Back at her hotel to pack an overnight bag, she called home for the first time. Dashiell answered on the second ring. It was early morning in New York.

'I miss you,' he said. 'When are you coming back?'

She laughed. 'I've only just got here. How's Bethany?'

He filled the conversation with funny stories about their daughter. She'd spat out her first taste of ice cream but loved the bitterness of olives. The zoo had terrified her, but the sharks in the aquarium had not. At bedtime, she'd kissed Etta's photograph with a smack of her lips.

'And how about you?' Dashiell's tone was gentle. He understood what it had cost her to return.

'I haven't been to Nate's grave yet.' Tears pricked the back of her eyes, hot and sudden. She hadn't planned to say that. But the guilt she felt had risen to the surface on hearing his voice.

'You'll go when you can,' he said, non-judgemental and reassuring. Full of his trademark warmth. 'I know you, Etta.'

It was true. He did. But he didn't know everything. Like how being back in London made the blood in her veins buzz with excitement. Or how much she'd missed the noise and dirt and chaos of her city.

'I'd better go now,' she said. Even though she still had half an hour before Toni collected her. Dashiell loved New York. Her thoughts felt like a betrayal.

'I love you,' he said. And then he was gone.

9

Wednesday

Saul hadn't left the flat all day. Except to buy credit for his phone and a pint of milk. He'd slipped down the back steps around lunchtime. There and back in less than ten minutes. On his way home, his heart had lifted at the sight of a woman. She was standing by the cliff steps, opposite their flat. Hair blown everywhere in the wind. But it wasn't Gloria. Just a stranger wearing the same coat.

He'd thought about making Gloria a birthday cake. Three layers of chocolate. Or maybe jam and cream. But she hardly ate a thing these days. A waste of fucking money, if you asked him. His stomach rumbled. Six o'clock. It was still early enough for her to make it home for fish and chips.

The wind was whipping in from the sea. A weather warning had been issued for the south-east. Saul wondered if the police tents on the island were strong enough to withstand it. Were the bodies still there? Or had they been bagged up and were sitting in a mortuary somewhere?

The letter box rattled. A familiar *rat-a-tat-tat.* Their secret code. About fucking time. He should play it cool. Make her wait. But he couldn't help himself. He ran down the stairs to welcome his mother home.

Disappointment filled his mouth, bitter as seawater. It wasn't his mother, but Etta Fitzroy and that other detective. He stared at them both, couldn't speak.

Etta was carrying a parcel of fish and chips. It was wrapped in paper, grease spots beginning to show. He could smell vinegar. He wanted to throw it at her.

'We thought you might be hungry.' She smiled at him but her smile faltered when she noticed his expression. 'Is everything OK?'

He said nothing. Fixed his gaze on a spot behind her left shoulder. It was a technique he'd perfected at school. Or when talking to social services or representatives from the local authority. Distanced, unemotional. Give nothing away.

DS Storm tried next. 'Can we come in? It's bloody freezing out here.' His gaze drifted to the streetlamp behind her. The garden gate. The holder for milk bottles by the front door.

He tried not to react but he couldn't help himself. His face crumpled, now more of a boy than a man. His mouth dried. He sank to his knees. Lying in grass that hadn't been mown for months was his mother's mobile phone.

Saul lunged for it. The screen was cracked. It hadn't been cracked yesterday. He was certain of that. He pressed the buttons, but the phone remained off. He cast around wildly, searching for clues. He couldn't feel the rain. Or the wind. He couldn't feel anything. Except a burning need to see what other traces she might have left.

He didn't have to look far. Beneath the yellow rose bush that she loved so much was her purse. The leather was worn and the catch was loose. He opened it. A fifty-pence piece. One plastic clip-on earring. And a worry doll made of pipe cleaners he'd once made her at school.

From a far-away place, he could hear voices. They were repeating his name over and over again. He ignored them. On his hands and knees, he groped in the rain and the darkness. Finally, there it was. Her key.

'She came home,' he said. His voice sounded like bits of broken metal.

'Come inside, Saul.' Etta helped him up, and

he allowed himself to be led upstairs like a small child.

Toni was in the bathroom. She returned with a towel so thin in places that it was almost see-through. While he sat with limp arms, she rubbed his wet hair as a mother might.

Etta appeared with a mug of tea, sweetened with three spoonfuls of sugar. She crouched beside him. 'What's going on, Saul?'

He could hear his father's voice. *Don't even look at them, boy.* The slap on the back of his head. Even though he was dead, Solomon Anguish's presence lingered in the flat. The police were not to be trusted. *Pigs. Filthy lying bastards. The enemy, every fucking one of them.*

There was a blackness inside Saul, as thick as tar. He felt it although he didn't fully understand it. It lent him strength and courage. A watchful cunning. He didn't need anyone's help. He could find his mother on his own. He was smarter than all of his friends. And dangerous, if he needed to be. He wasn't afraid of anything.

But a tiny voice of doubt tormented him. He didn't know where to start looking. Because he was a nobody. Just a council flat kid on his own. What if she was hurt? Lying somewhere in the darkness and the rain by herself. His memory threw him back to the previous night. Something had woken him. He thought he'd heard the scream of an owl, animals outside their front door. But what if that had been his mother?

He was aware of the women talking in soft voices. The crackle of a police radio. His duvet was tucked over his knees. He heard Etta say, 'There are no other relatives.' He wanted to speak up then, but his tongue felt too thick in his mouth.

'My mother . . .'

In an instant, Etta was beside him. 'Where is she?'

He shook his head. Stupid question. 'I don't know.'

'She didn't come home last night?'

'No. Or today.' He tried to smile, but his skin felt stretched. Like it belonged to somebody else. 'It's her birthday.'

The two women huddled in the corner. He knew before they told him what the outcome would be. Gloria was an adult. Gloria had a record for petty theft and public disorder. Gloria had been missing for less than twenty-four hours. Gloria was not worth anyone's time. They would do nothing.

'But there were signs of a struggle,' he heard Etta say to DS Storm.

DS Storm's response was blunt. 'Or she was drunk.' They whispered some more. Eventually,

DS Storm touched him lightly on the arm. 'Is there anyone we can call for you?'

He shook his head, refusing to look at her. There wasn't. Saul had always been on his own.

When they had gone, he tipped the fish and chips that Etta had left for him onto a plate. Then he threw it at the wall. The plate fractured into half a dozen pieces, batter and lumps of haddock everywhere. Then he punched his fist into the plaster, as he had seen his father do. Then he made a plan.

A couple of hours later, Saul was dressed in a warm jumper and jeans. He had a torch in his rucksack. Gloria's purse. And a knife he'd found in the kitchen drawer. In his pocket was the list he'd made earlier.

As he prepared to leave, he heard a light tapping sound coming from the kitchen. At first, Saul thought it was a branch from the tree outside, moving in the wind. Mrs Mallory, who lived next door, was always complaining that it needed cutting back.

But the kitchen also had a back door. It opened onto concrete steps that ran down the back of their building to a private garden. He almost didn't answer it. But when he stood, half hidden in the shadows, he glimpsed her outline in the security light.

Rivulets of water tracked down her raincoat. Her eyes – blue and brown – were wary, but friendly. She gave him a tentative smile. 'I couldn't leave you on your own to figure this out. Anyway, I owe you, don't I?'

And Saul opened the door to let in Etta Fitzroy.

10

Wednesday

Although Etta believed in rules, she'd never worried too much about following them. In any case, she was no longer an official employee of the Metropolitan Police. She was a consultant. Freelance. She could make her own decisions.

Even so, she knew DS Toni Storm would not approve of her actions. Toni had always insisted it was important not to let professional and personal boundaries blur. As she hurried along the rainy cobbles of the Old Town, Etta kept her head down. Toni had gone to meet a friend at one of the nearby waterside pubs. 'You're welcome to join us.' But Etta had declined, blaming her jet-lag. 'If you're sure,' said Toni. And Etta had smiled and said she would have an early night.

It was the gift box on the living-room table that had made up her mind. It was badly wrapped with too much Sellotape. A child trying to impress his mother. Her heart had ached for the loneliness in Saul's face. Their dusty flat. The general air of neglect. He might be eighteen, full of bravado, but he wasn't a man. Not yet.

'What do you want?'

His tone was rough. Almost angry. She didn't blame him. As far as he was concerned, the police had washed their hands of his mother.

'To help.'

He'd turned from her then, but hadn't closed the door. She'd taken that as an invitation to follow him in.

For a few moments, neither of them spoke. Then Saul said, 'I'm going to the pub. She was on a shift there last night.'

It was as good a place to start as any.

The rain was keeping all but the most dedicated punters away. The Mayflower was at the opposite end of the Old Town to the Peterboat, Toni's dinner spot. Even so, Etta was nervous about being seen. Saul kept to the shadows, and she followed his example.

The pub was almost empty except for a couple of youngsters, playing pool. The room smelled of stale beer and chips. A man – late fifties, but he might have been older – was wiping down a table. His face lit up when he saw Saul.

'All right, son. How's life treating you?' The man gave Etta a curious look, but didn't speak to her.

Saul gave a sort of half-shrug that could have meant anything. 'Have you seen Gloria?'

The man – who was called Barry – snorted. 'I was going to ask you the same question. She went out for a cigarette in the middle of her shift last night. Never came back.'

Saul tensed his jaw. 'Did you go outside and look for her?'

'Course I bloody did. She left me short-staffed, didn't she? And I rang her. Several times.'

Although she'd planned to keep quiet, Etta couldn't stop herself from filling in the gaps. Once a police officer, always a police officer. 'What time was this?'

The man eyed her. 'About nine thirty. Perhaps a bit later.'

'Can you be any more precise?'

Barry dug a cocktail stick into a back tooth and waggled it. When he removed it, an unidentifiable piece of food clung to its tip. 'No.'

'Do you have any CCTV cameras on the premises?'

He dropped his cocktail stick in a bin behind the bar. He folded his arms, unimpressed. 'I don't mean to be rude, but what's it to you?'

Etta bristled at his attitude but bit her lip. Saul spoke up. 'We're worried about Gloria, that's all. Etta's helping me look for her.'

Barry snorted again. 'She'll turn up. She always does.' But his eyes slid away when he said it.

A woman with dyed blonde hair and dark roots walked out of a door marked PRIVATE. She was wearing a red jacket and carrying a plastic handbag in the same colour.

'You all right if I head off now, Baz?'

He gave a good-natured grunt. 'Go on, then. But make sure you're on time tomorrow.' She rolled her eyes. 'I mean it, Rachel.'

Rachel blew him a kiss and disappeared in a cloud of perfume. Etta caught Saul's eye and they followed her out.

'Excuse me,' Etta called to the woman, who'd stopped outside the pub for a puff on her vape.

'What do you want? I don't speak to police.' Etta's mouth fell open and the woman laughed. 'I can smell it a mile off.'

'Do you know my mum? Gloria Anguish?' Saul asked.

Rachel looked Saul up and down. 'Poor sod.' Saul's face fell and the woman took pity on him. 'I was just kidding. I do know Gloria, but she can be a bit . . .'

'A bit what?' said Etta.

57

'Chaotic. Disorganized. Unreliable.' Rachel counted out each word on her fingers. 'Oh, and drunk.' She smiled at Saul. 'What's she done now? Lost her purse and keys again? Been sick in her handbag?'

Saul was silent, but Etta could sense his distress. 'She's missing,' she said softly.

Rachel's body language changed immediately. A hand covered her mouth. Her eyes, large and brown, were full of compassion. 'I'm sorry. I didn't know.'

'Did you see her last night?' Etta could see that Saul was in no state to ask questions.

When Rachel nodded, her whole body moved too. 'Yes, we were on the same shift.'

'Did she mention any plans she might have made with friends? Or a lover, perhaps?'

'That woman wasn't going home to anyone except Saul. She told me that herself.'

This revelation was deeply concerning. Etta glanced at the young man. His face was drawn and pale. 'Was it mostly regulars in last night?'

Rachel tutted. 'It was quiet. Between you and me, I'm worried Barry's going to sack one of us. But there were a couple of men I didn't recognize. Gloria served them. One was a redhead. And I think she bummed a cigarette from the other one.

58

I remember him because he had a deep scar down his cheek.'

Ting. 'Did you notice if he went outside with her?'

'Yeah, I think so. Gloria winked at me as she went past. But he came back in a few minutes later. He and his friend left shortly afterwards.'

Saul glanced at Etta. She spoke again. 'Did you happen to get a name for these men?'

Rachel slid her vape into her handbag. The rain was heavier now and a mist clung to everything. 'No, but one of them was driving a van.'

Etta held her breath as Saul asked exactly what she'd been thinking. 'Did you see it? What about a registration number? Did it have a logo or name on the outside?'

'As a matter of fact, I did. I saw them drive off in it when Baz sent me out to look for Gloria. It was white and from the fish shop on the high street.'

In the glow of the streetlamp, they watched Rachel head across the footbridge towards home. As Saul turned to leave, something glinted in the dimness. He crouched, his fingers groping in a dirty puddle. He frowned. This wasn't an accident. It was a message from Gloria. Lying in the water was the only valuable item his mother had never pawned. Her wedding ring.

11

Wednesday

It was too dark to see now. Saul fumbled with his torch and shone it onto the cliff steps, slippery with rain. He didn't feel much like talking. But the police officer who wasn't a police officer wouldn't shut up. He wished she'd go away.

'The fish shop will be closed tonight, but we can go there at first light. Or perhaps we should ask around the fishermen on the jetty.'

He didn't answer but concentrated on keeping his balance in the wind. When a storm blew in from the sea, it was powerful. It made him feel vulnerable, exposed to the elements. For a brief flash, he fantasized about shoving her down the steps. The silence would be a relief. But he pushed that thought away. She was only trying to help him find his mother.

At the top of the cliff, he turned to her. The path was deserted. 'You'd better head off.'

Although he was taller than she was, it didn't occur to him to walk her back. She was the adult.

She looked uncertain. 'Saul, is there anyone I can call for you?'

There was no one. But she didn't need to know that. 'I'm not a kid.' He sounded angrier than he meant to. But it made him defensive, always having to explain himself.

'I know that.' An expression close to pity crossed her face. It inflamed him. She had no idea what it was to grow up in a household like his. He'd had no parents to protect him. Gloria didn't know how to. It was why she needed protecting herself. Etta spoke again. God, she never stopped speaking. 'Let me know if you change your mind.'

Saul gave a sort of half-shrug. Etta gave him a look he couldn't read. 'Goodnight, then.' She set off back down the cliff steps in the direction of her guest house. In seconds, the darkness had swallowed her up.

Inside the flat, Saul's breath was visible in the cold air. He boiled the kettle, determined to head back out once he'd warmed up. But as soon as he sat on the sofa, a tiredness crept into his bones. He drank his tea, switched off the lamp and allowed his eyes to close. He'd sleep first, just for an hour or so.

When he woke up, Saul couldn't breathe. It took him a few seconds to gather himself. And then it hit him. He couldn't breathe because someone's gloved hand was pressing against his mouth.

Instinct drove him to struggle. But it was impossible. It felt as if a heavy weight had been placed on his body. He couldn't move his arms or legs. Panic thrummed through him. He struggled again, but it was no use. Saul Anguish was a prisoner. He blinked into the darkness but it was difficult to see anything. He was dimly aware of shapes moving around him.

And then a voice in his ear, low and threatening. 'If you'd like to see Gloria again, we've got a suggestion. Stay away from things that are none of your fucking business.'

Saul tried to speak but the hand across his mouth wouldn't let him. Another voice, gravelly and with the hint of an accent, said, 'Stop asking questions and get your friends to stop asking questions too. Then we'll let the stupid bitch go.'

A fist struck him. Pain – sharp, eye-watering – blossomed on the left side of his head. He bit his lip, determined not to give them the satisfaction of crying out. Saul felt himself falling into nothingness, his vision blurring at the edges. He tried to cling on to consciousness. He had no idea who these men were, but he had questions. So many questions.

Without warning, the pressure on his body lifted. He sensed a change in the atmosphere of the room. The sound of footsteps, the slam of the front door.

With his usual stubbornness, Saul forced himself off the sofa. The room swam and he thought he might be sick. He pressed a palm against the wall and edged his way to the window. Dizziness threatened to overwhelm him, but he made himself walk.

Below the flat, the street was dark and silent. Even the streetlamps were off. In the distance, Saul could see the red tail lights of a van as it turned the corner. A white van.

He touched his fingertips to his temple, the pain making him wince. When he pulled his hand away, it was stained with blood. In the artificial light of the bathroom mirror, he was pale and hollow-eyed. A bruise was already forming on his temple. But Saul didn't weep at the violence he'd been subjected to. He didn't weep at the knowledge that strangers had invaded his home.

He burned with rage.

When he had cleaned himself up, he went into the kitchen and unplugged Gloria's phone. It had been dead when he'd found it but now it was charged. He hoped it would provide the key to her whereabouts. Gloria had always been casual about security. He'd known her passcode for as long as he could remember. Although he was pretty sure she didn't know that. For the first time in his life, he was glad of her slapdash attitude.

He scrolled through her messages. Several from Barry at the pub. A couple from people he didn't recognize, but nothing of interest. He listened to her voicemail. Checked her dialled numbers. He frowned, sure there must be a clue hidden somewhere.

And then he found it. The Notes app on her phone was open. Several numbers and letters had been written down. He gazed at them, trying to puzzle out what they might mean. He had been good at maths at school, and wondered if it was some kind of hidden code. But that wasn't Gloria's style. Something niggled at his brain, but it remained out of reach. He took a screenshot and sent it to himself.

He shivered, delayed shock hitting him. The bastards had forced their way in through the back door. He spent half an hour sweeping up broken glass from the window. Then he taped a piece of cardboard against the hole. He didn't feel like going out again now, but he was too fired up to go to sleep. In the back of the cupboard, he found an old sachet of Cup-a-Soup. He drank it in front of the television, old game shows on repeat. By the time dawn had broken, Saul Anguish had a plan.

12

Thursday

The seagulls were so loud they woke her up. As a city dweller, Etta Fitzroy was more used to car alarms and sirens. She let out a groan and rolled over. It was early, a faint light visible through the crack in the curtains.

Toni had still been at the pub when Etta had returned, soaked from the rain. She'd showered and climbed into bed, too tired to even ring home. She'd lain in the darkness, listening to the waves. Thinking about the boy with the white-blond hair and the haunted eyes. Her last conscious thought before sleep claimed her was of Saul. She vowed to speak to The Boss in the morning. She would insist on help to find his mother.

Which was why she was surprised to wake up and discover the message. She propped herself up against the lumpy pillow and read it twice: GLORIA'S BEEN IN TOUCH. SHE WAS SLEEPING

OFF HER HANGOVER. THANKS FOR YOUR HELP. SAUL.

It was a brush-off, if ever she'd heard one. She read it again, confused. It didn't say that Gloria was home, although she presumed his mother was safe. Her fingers hovered over the dial button. She could call him, just to be sure. But something stopped her. Saul didn't like strangers. And he didn't like police. She was close to being both.

Over breakfast, Toni detailed their plans for the day. They would return to the site where the bodies had been found and confirm that the island was properly secured. And then they would head back to London again.

'What about Saul?' The words were out before she could stop them.

'What about him?' Toni buttered a slice of toast. When she saw Etta's face, her own expression softened. 'I know you feel responsible for him, but he's old enough to look after himself.'

And what could she say to that?

A mist hung over the island. All of the bodies had now been bagged and removed. Toni was busy co-ordinating operations with the local police. Etta, feeling out of place, wandered to the edge of the shore, gazing across the estuary.

Why was she here? She should be at home in New York with her family.

On impulse, she typed out a message to her sister, Nina. The two women were in regular contact and had last seen each other at Christmas. But that was almost a year ago. It would be good to catch up this afternoon, if Nina was free.

Not for the first time, she wondered if Gloria was safely home yet. Saul was too old for Etta to intervene, but he was still young. A boy, really. Why did he stick around that dump of a flat? He was intelligent and observant. The world was his for the taking. But it didn't take a detective to work it out. Saul felt responsible for his mother.

A rat scampered through the undergrowth, bigger than her foot. Even the rats in the New York subway were smaller than this one. The thought it might be riddled with disease made her shudder. According to the police radio, the colony of crabs had been located and contained. For now. Fortunately for Etta, they were on the other side of the island. Still, it didn't hurt to be cautious.

She watched the waves for a while, the ever-changing seascape and sky. Her eye was drawn to a rusty structure rising from the depths. It looked like something from *The War of the Worlds*, the science fiction novel by H. G. Wells. If she remembered correctly, the tower was called a Maunsell Fort. It was used to defend the estuary from invaders during the Second World War. With its spindly legs and boxy body, it made her think of an alien spacecraft. At its rear, she spotted an entry ladder leading down to the sea.

The sea forts had been decommissioned in the 1950s. Some of them had been used as pirate radio stations, which meant they broadcast without a licence. But this fort had long been abandoned to the elements. Its windows were still intact but chunks of its main structure had fallen into the waters below. She counted seven forts, collected around a central control tower. There was something eerie and otherworldly about them.

From behind the nearest fort, a fishing boat came into view, nets dangling over the side. But they were empty, no sign of that morning's catch. The two men in the boat stared at her as they chugged past. One of the men had a beard. The other had a deep scar running from his ear to his nose.

Rachel's words replayed in her brain. *I remember him because he had a deep scar down his cheek.*

Too late, Etta reacted. 'Hey!' She waved her arms at the men but they either didn't see or didn't care. She ran along the shoreline, trying to catch their attention. But, within moments, they had disappeared from view.

Frustrated, Etta turned away from the water. What else could she do? Toni had no idea that she'd met up with Saul the previous night. And something made Etta keep it to herself. Toni motioned to her from across the scrubby vegetation. She pushed the sighting from her mind. It was time to go back to London

The Boss was pacing the floor of his office at New Scotland Yard. DS Toni Storm caught Etta's eye. It was clear that something was up.

'Is everything OK?'

'No. It's not.' He explained why. One of the missing women was the daughter of an extraordinarily wealthy businessman. A social media influencer with a public profile. Now that her body had been discovered, he was demanding answers about her death.

'Can't blame him,' said Etta.

'What do we know about her situation?' Toni was flicking through a bundle of witness statements on The Boss's desk.

The Boss rubbed his hand across his chin. 'She went to a nightclub in Spitalfields. Told her friends she was popping outside to get some air. Never seen again.'

'Drugs?'

'Probably. Except no one would admit to that. And it's too late for toxicology tests now.' He grimaced. 'There's not enough left of her.'

'What about the others?' Etta remembered what he'd said about all those missing people in the photos on his wall. There was seemingly no connection between them except drugs. And drugs – cocaine, heroin, weed – did not care about how much money you had, your skin colour, gender or age.

'Drugs, you mean?' The Boss shrugged. 'It's beginning to look that way, I suppose. We weren't looking for connections, to be honest. Not at the start. But you might have a point. I'll get some of the team to check their phone records again. See if there's a recurring contact number, a pager or mobile, that sort of thing.'

'Coffee?' Toni grinned at them both. 'I'm dying of thirst.'

While Toni was fetching their drinks, Etta sat opposite The Boss at his desk. His head was down, writing something, but he looked up and caught her staring.

'You OK?'

'What do you remember about Gloria Anguish?'

The Boss snorted. 'That she's a drunk. Although I heard she cleaned up her act years ago.'

Etta gave a non-committal shrug, sounding him out. 'Well, she sold his father's watch, so it would appear not.'

'People like that, you can't trust them, Etta. They deserve everything they get.' He wrinkled his nose as he spoke, as if he could smell something unpleasant. She looked at him through fresh eyes. *People like that.* Power had changed him. It sounded suspiciously like judgement to her.

'She needed the money.'

'We all need money. It doesn't mean we numb the pain with alcohol and take what isn't ours.'

'She went missing for two nights.'

'Pissed?'

'I don't know.' She wanted to share her concerns. That it all seemed too much of a coincidence. That her gut instinct was telling her that Saul was lying about his mother's safety. But then The Boss rolled his eyes, as if Gloria's life didn't matter much to him at all. 'And is she still missing?'

'I don't think so.'

'No harm done then.' The Boss put down his pen, the Anguish family forgotten. 'Back in a jiffy.'

The office was silent. Through the open door, she could hear the voices of police officers and civilian staff. Etta thought of smug officials in their expensive offices. People like The Boss who had enjoyed a lifetime of privilege. A warm bed. Clean clothes. A fridge bursting with expensive cheeses and the best cuts of meat. The contents of his wine cellar worth more than a month's salary.

And then she thought about Saul – and Gloria, too – in their unheated flat. Mildew on the walls. No food in the cupboards. Husband and father dead. And no one to care.

For a brief moment, Etta fought with her conscience. But the decision had been made in the rain of the Old Town last night. She jumped up from her chair and began to search, opening drawers and cupboards. Praying that no one could see what she was up to. Taking something that didn't belong to her.

By the time Toni returned with three steaming mugs of coffee, Etta was sitting back in her chair. As much of a thief as Saul.

13

Thursday

Saul was up and dressed before daybreak. By the time he reached the jetty, fishermen in oilskins were laying out their nets. Buckets of herring were being hefted ashore. Cockles and whelks. And dozens of kite-shaped thornback rays. The whole place stank of fish guts.

The young man hid in the early-morning shadows. His eyes scanned the vehicles parked close to the cockle sheds. But none matched Rachel's description of the van. He listened to the men calling to each other, the joy of honest work.

Across the estuary, a fiery sun was inching above the horizon. He rubbed his hands together in the cold air. His stomach rumbled. He'd kill for a bacon sandwich and a mug of tea.

Just as Saul was growing bored of waiting, the rumble of an engine caught his attention. He watched a van cruise down the slipway and park near one of the boats. It was branded with the same logo as one of the fishmongers on the high street. Exactly as Rachel had said.

His heart thumped faster. It didn't mean it was the same van. There was probably more than one. Almost definitely. But something about it tickled his memory. On a hunch, he pulled his phone from his pocket to check. His heart thumped faster still.

Apart from one missing digit, the registration plate of the van was a match. Its numbers and letters were the same as the ones Gloria had saved into her phone. Except the final letter was not there. Which meant his mother had been in a hurry when she'd left behind this clue. Or in grave danger.

A man with a scar on his cheek stepped out of the van. He spoke briefly to one of the fishermen, red-headed and bearded. Saul's immediate reaction was to approach him. To beat the truth from him. But he'd been warned once to stay away. And he wasn't ready to show his hand yet. He would watch and wait.

Luck was on Saul's side that morning. Instead of climbing back into his van, the man began walking along the sea wall. Saul followed him at a safe distance until he reached the bridge that led to the island.

Saul frowned, knowing it was off-limits. A police cordon was still in place and officers were on site. But the man didn't cross the bridge. Instead he jumped off the sea wall into a boat that had been waiting, hidden from view.

Burning with curiosity, Saul noticed it was the same boat he'd seen on the jetty. Its skipper was the same one the man with the scar had been talking to. Why hadn't they launched with the rest of the fleet? Did they have something to hide?

Pleased he had planned for just such a moment, Saul dug into his rucksack for an old pair of binoculars. He'd bought them at a car boot sale a few months earlier, but hadn't expected them to prove so useful. He adjusted the settings until the interior of the boat was in focus. The man with the scar handed over a brown envelope. It looked like it was stuffed with cash. The boat set off at a fast clip and Saul watched it follow the curve of the bay.

He ran down the beach, determined to follow its progress. He watched until it was further out to sea. Then it seemed to come to a halt. Saul squinted, trying for a better look. The boat had stalled in the middle of the estuary, close to the sea forts. Saul had learned about them at school. To him, they looked like something out of *Star Wars*.

'What are you up to?' He whispered the words to himself. High above him, a flock of brent-geese flew inland in a V-shaped formation. Saul watched them go, enjoying the spectacle of these impressive birds. The sky was streaked with pale golds and oranges, a promise of morning.

When Saul turned his attention back to the boat, the man with the scar was gone. *That's impossible.* But true. He squinted through his binoculars, but the only person on board was the red-headed skipper.

Perhaps he was seasick, lying below deck. Or had fallen overboard. But the relaxed behaviour of the skipper suggested this wasn't the case.

Saul kept his binoculars trained on the boat. Minutes passed. But the boat stayed in position, anchored to the seabed. He wondered what Etta would make of this. He'd have liked to discuss it with her but that was out of the question.

The sun was now fully risen, its reflection on the waves like scattered diamonds. But there was no heat in the day yet. He shifted, uncomfortable with waiting in the chill of the morning air.

Saul was close to giving up when something interesting caught his eye. A flicker of movement, at first. Nothing more than that. He held his breath, not sure if he'd imagined it, but not daring to look away. No, Saul definitely hadn't imagined it. Because descending the ladder of the sea fort was a pair of heavy black boots.

14

Thursday

The restaurant was quiet, which wasn't surprising given it was a midweek afternoon. Etta fiddled with her napkin. Nina had a habit of reading her mind, and she didn't want to answer awkward questions. Not today.

'Sorry I'm late. The Tube was delayed.' Her younger sister shrugged off her coat. Tiny droplets of moisture clung to its fibres. Nina ran a hand through her hair and grinned at Etta. 'You look knackered.' She could always rely on Nina to tell her the truth.

They ordered plates of spaghetti with clams and large glasses of white wine. Nina chattered non-stop about her son Max and her house and her new job at an animal charity.

'Anyway, enough about me. How are *you*?' She always did that, put the emphasis on *you*. It was a loaded question. Etta bit into a slice of garlicky bread to avoid answering it. 'Etta?'

She forced a smile. 'Fine, fine.'

'*Are* you?'

She swallowed a mouthful of wine. 'Yes,' she said simply. 'Or rather as fine as I'm ever going to be.'

Nina knew immediately what she meant. 'Have you been to see him yet?'

Tears pricked the back of Etta's eyes. 'Not yet.'

Her sister placed a hand on hers. 'We've been looking after his grave. There's nothing to be afraid of.'

But there was. Etta was afraid of guilt. She was afraid of leaving him behind again. She was afraid that she would never have another child. Some women thought she should be grateful. One of the grandmothers at playgroup in New York had patted her on the arm. 'It's God's will, sweetie. At least you've got one. Be grateful for that.' But there should be two coats hanging on the peg. Two pairs of shoes by the front door. Two little faces to kiss goodnight.

Etta changed the subject. What good would it do to dwell on it? Years had passed now, and she was still grieving. She would always grieve. Instead, she made Nina laugh with stories of her mishaps in the big city. Their tiny but expensive apartment. How Dashiell had locked himself in the museum he worked in overnight by accident.

All too soon, it was time to say goodbye. Nina made her promise to come for dinner before she left. 'Everyone misses you.' She kissed Etta on both cheeks and grabbed her shoulders with both hands. 'Look after yourself.' And then she was gone, back to her busy life and her family.

Etta paid the bill and wandered into the afternoon. The sky was losing its colour, fading into dusk. She walked through south-east London's streets on auto-pilot, her old stomping ground. Past the bright lights of the shops. Past the pubs she used to visit at weekends and after work. The cafes for brunch with her friends. The wide expanse of Greenwich Park. She walked until she found herself in an under-the-radar corner of the city. And then, outside a familiar set of gates.

She hesitated, not sure if she had the emotional strength to go in. But she squared her shoulders and forced herself onwards. Away from the main pathways was a quieter part of the cemetery. The stones were much smaller here. There were teddy bears and windmills. Echoes of what might have been. She could remember the inscriptions of love and loss by heart.

The children's graveyard. The place where her son Nate was buried. Two simple words carved into the headstone below his name: *Born asleep*. Born dead, more like.

She told herself off for her dark thoughts and pulled her coat tightly around her body. But it was no defence against the wind. The air felt icy, as if an overnight frost was on its way. The afternoon was dimming rapidly now and she blinked into the shadows. The trees that bordered the cemetery were black shapes in the twilight. But she wasn't frightened of the dead who were buried here. In her experience, the living were far more dangerous.

Nate's grave was tucked away in the corner beneath an oak tree. Even though she hadn't visited it for two years, she remembered exactly where it was. Nina had been as good as her word. The grass around it was neatly trimmed. A sprig of baby's breath poked out of a vase, tiny white petals in the gloom.

As she grew closer, something unexpected caught her eye. Her brain tried to untangle what she was seeing, but it took her a moment. And then the pieces of the puzzle fell into place.

Nate's headstone had been vandalized. Her precious boy's resting place had been violated by a stranger. A heat rose inside her, a red-hot mist. But it wasn't graffiti. There were no streaks of paint or sprayed-on slogans. She took a step closer, and the smell made her gag. It was rotting flesh and saltwater. It reminded her of another time and place, although Mr Silver was long since dead.

Etta crouched down in the grass, fighting the urge to be sick. Then she gathered herself and took in the scene. Several crabs had been smashed to pieces on his grave. Their innards were smeared across the grey marble. Fragments of shell were scattered far and wide. Half a dozen claws had been cracked open and the meat left to rot. The carcasses were running with maggots.

Could a bird have done this? She didn't think so. The destruction was too widespread. It was true that the cemetery wasn't far from the River Thames. But this was a deliberate act. It wasn't a coincidence. And these crabs were the same size and species as the ones on the nature reserve. It was only an hour's drive here from the Essex estuary. Again, she was reminded of her past. Of Mr Silver and the rabbit skeletons he'd left at the scenes of his abductions.

It was a message. Had to be.

But if that was the case, who was sending it? And what were they trying to say? More importantly, how had they linked her to Nate's grave so quickly?

She ran through several theories, discounting

them all. Then her brain snagged on a memory. *The Times* newspaper had profiled her after Mr Silver's death. She'd been persuaded by a journalist, against her better judgement, to be photographed at the cemetery. *The human face of policing*, the journalist had said. *The tragedy behind the investigation* and all that. *From one grief-stricken mother to another.*

Someone somewhere had let her name slip to the wrong people. And now they were trying to scare her with sick tactics from her previous investigation.

She shivered, cold now the sun had gone down. Frightened too. It felt like a warning.

As the shock began to recede, Etta fought back the tears rising inside her. How dare someone desecrate her son's grave? But it felt more personal than that. It was designed to scare her off. For the first time in a while, she felt vulnerable.

But if she – a former police officer – felt this way, what about the boy? She wondered if Saul had been targeted too. Gut instinct told her it was not just possible, but likely.

For a moment, she allowed herself to indulge in daydreams about her son. He'd be seven now, tall as a weed. Playing football. Reading by himself. Growing up. What colour would his hair be? Would he prefer peas or carrots? Would he look like her? She closed her eyes, tears wetting her lashes. *Stop it, Etta*, she thought. This was pointless speculation. She would never know the answers.

Her boy was lost to her, somewhere in the dark. But Saul wasn't lost. If her son had lived, he might have needed help one day. She hoped he'd have found it. As a mother, she felt compelled to act. To protect the angry boy with a darkness about him. Her maternal instinct was powerful, at times it overwhelmed her. But she wanted to help him. It was too late for Nate. For Saul, there was still time to change the direction of his life.

Etta did not allow herself to think of more than practicalities. Instead, she cleared the remains of the crabs from her son's grave. Then she caught a taxi to Fenchurch Street station and bought a ticket to Leigh-on-Sea.

She would work out what to say to Saul when she got there.

15

Thursday

Saul had spent most of the day pacing the streets of the Old Town. He'd returned to the Mayflower, his mother's workplace, but they'd heard nothing. He'd called every single one of her friends. And most of her enemies too. He'd walked along the coast to the Victorian bus shelter where she sometimes got drunk. He'd obsessively monitored her phone for new messages. But there was still no sign of Gloria and he was running out of ideas.

It was dark now and he didn't know what to do next. He prowled the flat, unable to settle. A part of him wondered if the men would pay him a visit again that night. Just in case, he'd hidden an old baseball bat under his bed. In some ways, he wished they would. He'd be better prepared this time. No one caught him out twice.

He mulled over the events of the day. But he kept returning to one fact, replaying it in his mind. That pair of old boots, climbing down the sea fort's ladder. What had the man with the scar been doing up there? Those forts were closed to the public, decommissioned decades ago. *What if his mother was being held captive there?* He shook his head. Of course she wasn't. It was too risky, out there in the middle of the sea. But it would be an excellent hiding place. And a tiny voice repeated the question. *What if? What if? What if?*

He gazed out across the estuary, at the lights dotting the horizon. An idea came to him. A stupid, dangerous idea. At first, he dismissed it. But it kept poking at him until it became impossible to ignore. Why did he care so much about rescuing Gloria anyway? She was a drunk who'd neglected him his whole life. But every now and again, he remembered flashes of tenderness from her. How it felt to be held by his mother when she was well. And surely any mother – however useless – was better than no mother at all.

In the kitchen drawer, Saul found the torch they used when they couldn't afford electricity. And a sharp-bladed bread knife. From the cupboard, he grabbed a tattered rope he'd scavenged from the beach. He put on an old oilskin coat of Solomon's they hadn't got round to throwing away. And then Saul Anguish headed out into the night.

It was early evening, but the cold weather meant there was hardly anybody about. Saul hurried past the public gardens and down the steps that cut into the cliff. The tide was in and he could hear the rush of the water. Then he was heading to the harbour where most of the fishing boats were moored at night.

A handful of people were walking along the pavement, chatting and laughing. They were on their way to the pubs and restaurants in the Old Town. Saul pressed himself into the shadows but no one paid any attention to him. Mr Silver had once taught him how to blend into the night. To become invisible. A nobody. It was time to do that now.

Down by the water's edge, the cockle boats clanked and bobbed in the darkness. He could make out the shape of several large machines. But they were still and silent. The port was deserted, the crews gone until morning. In the near distance, he heard the approach of the train. Saul slid between the machinery until he came to a small boat called *The Mary-Lou*. It was tied to a metal ring on the jetty by a rope.

With a glance to make sure no one was watching, Saul began to tug at the knot. His fingers were cold and the rope was thick. He took the knife from the rucksack and began to saw at the fibres. After what seemed like forever, the rope split and Saul grabbed hold of one end. Then he jumped into the boat and picked up the oars. They made a soft splash as they cut through the water.

At first, Saul was delighted with his success. It had been easier than he thought. He felt a rush of joy at being afloat in the inky darkness. With a clear plan of action in mind. But the current was stronger than he'd anticipated and his arms quickly grew tired. The wind and the rain battered his face, making it difficult to see. And although Saul knew how to row, he was not sure how to navigate.

It was difficult to pinpoint when he realized he was in trouble. It might have been when the first wave crested the boat, soaking his legs. It might have been when the clouds hid the moon, his only source of light. It might have been when he could no longer see the sea forts. Just miles of empty water.

He forced himself to take deep breaths, trying not to panic. He looked about the stolen boat for a life-jacket. But the storage hatch was locked. Fumbling in his pocket, he pulled out his phone. But he was too far from the shore to get a signal.

He was too far from anything except the possibility of drowning.

Think, Saul. Think. He was a resourceful boy, one of the smartest in his year at school. He trawled his brain for any useful scraps of knowledge. The wind was gaining strength and the waves tossed the boat up and down. It would not take much to throw Saul into its freezing depths.

Saul was now seriously frightened. He could swim, yes. But it wouldn't take long for hypothermia to set in. And he had no idea how long he'd have the strength to stay afloat.

It was as if time stood still. Saul was at the mercy of the elements. He was almost resigned to his fate, preparing for his death. The boat gave another violent lurch and a wave hit Saul in the face. He swallowed a mouthful of saltwater, choking at its bitterness. Tears of regret and frustration spilled down his cheeks.

Perhaps it was the shock of the cold, but being hit by the wave sharpened his senses. With freezing fingers, he wiped away the tears and seawater. Then he felt around the floor of the boat, searching for his rucksack. It was soaked through, but he snatched it up, muttering a prayer.

The odds had been against Saul for all of his life. He wasn't about to give up now. He was going to fight for every chance – or die trying. Because Saul Anguish was determined to live. And he'd remembered something that might just save him.

16

Thursday

The train sped past the ruins of a castle and into the mouth of the estuary. Etta could smell the sea as soon as she walked out of the station. The tide was in and she paused, watching the rise and fall of the waves. The sound soothed her, but the sense of peace was short-lived.

A feeling of anxiety had settled into the pit of her stomach. It felt as heavy as a pile of stones. The vandalism of Nate's grave was a clear message. They were coming after her. And, if that was the case, they'd be coming after Saul too.

She hadn't told Toni or The Boss where she was going. They weren't interested in a woman like Gloria Anguish. In fairness to them, she could understand why. They were busy people with a backlog of cases and not enough resources. In their eyes, no crime had been committed. And Gloria was home now, wasn't she? So why did Etta feel so uneasy?

Taking a deep breath, she pulled out her phone and dialled Saul's number. Men and women with dark coats and umbrellas swarmed around her. The last of the early-evening commuters, spilling out of the station. A man bumped into her, making her stumble. 'Sorry,' he said, although he didn't sound it. It made her think of the New York subway. Of her own little family. A pang of homesickness knocked the air from her lungs.

Saul's phone went immediately to voicemail. She swore under her breath. She would have to climb the hill to his flat instead.

Etta started to trudge up Belton Way, the steep road that curved away from the station. At the last minute, she changed direction, deciding to walk into the Old Town instead. She followed the straight line of the train tracks. Past the concrete steps that led down to the mud. Past the cockle sheds and fresh fish stalls, closed up for the night. Until she reached the hulking shape of the buoy near the jetty.

A fine drizzle coated her face. She hesitated, not sure whether to pay another visit to Gloria's pub or go straight to Saul's. While she made up her mind, her eyes roamed across the dark well of the estuary. She frowned, trying to make sense of what she was seeing. She blinked once. Twice. But no, her eyes were not playing tricks on her.

A light in the darkness was flashing on and off. She stood for a while and watched it, counting the beats. Three short pulses. Three longer ones. Three short ones. An SOS in Morse code.

When she was certain she wasn't mistaken, Etta didn't think twice. She dialled the emergency services. 'Coastguard, please.' She gave her location and a rough position of the distress signal. The call handler, calm and reassuring, promised a lifeboat would be launched within minutes.

As soon as she hung up, she tried Saul again. But he still didn't answer.

Her sense of uneasiness deepened. She didn't know why but something inside her told her to stay close by. To stand on the shoreline and watch the rescue unfold. Experience had taught her over the years that it was wise not to ignore her instincts.

She zipped up her coat and dug her hands into her pockets.

And then she waited.

17

Thursday

Saul's hands were now so cold he could no longer hold the torch. As it slid from his grip, a series of moving lights appeared in the distance.

He blinked, not sure if his mind was playing tricks on him. But the lights appeared to be getting closer. Through a loudhailer, a voice implored him to flash the torch again.

Saul did as he was asked, but the rain was blinding him. He peered into the darkness, but it was impossible to see how close they were.

And then they were upon him. A small orange lifeboat cutting through the surf. Two men wearing helmets and yellow jackets pulled him from his fishing boat. A third man was at the controls. Coughing, Saul collapsed with relief onto the deck. He was grateful to these volunteers who'd risked their lives to save his. And to the stranger who'd raised the alarm.

'Are you OK?' An older man with kind eyes

bent over him. He tucked an emergency foil blanket over Saul's shoulders.

. He nodded, but couldn't answer. Shock had stolen his voice. The man gave him a couple of squares of chocolate. 'Eat this. We'll have you back on dry land in no time.'

Saul crammed it into his mouth, the sweetness replacing the taste of salt. The man helped him into a life-jacket.

'Was there anyone else with you?'

He shook his head. *No.* 'But I was looking for someone.'

'Out on the water?'

'Yeah. My mother. I was trying to reach the sea forts. I think she's in one of them.'

The man laughed. 'No, champ. No one in their right mind would be out there on a night like this.'

'Not through choice.'

'And you're sure she's in there?'

'No.' He was honest. 'But what if I'm right?' He felt a surge of shame, but defiance too. 'I know it was stupid, but I had to try.'

The man – who had said his name was Frank – looked thoughtful. He placed a hand on Saul's shoulder. 'Don't move.' Then ignoring his own advice, Frank crossed the vessel, trying to keep upright. He shouted something to one of the rescue crew, who spoke into the radio. And then they were flying across the water at great speed.

The lifeboat was faster than anything Saul had experienced before. Waves crashed over the sides, but the boat remained stable, able to right itself. The noise was all-consuming. He closed his eyes, feeling sick, but not from the motion. Sick at the thought he might be right about Gloria. Or wrong.

The first sea fort was in complete darkness when it came into view. The lifeboat pulled up underneath the ladder and the skipper killed the engine. The man with the kind eyes stood up. 'Let's do it.'

'I'm coming with you,' said Saul.

'I don't think so,' said Frank.

'I have to.'

Frank looked like he was going to argue. Saul could guess what he was thinking. *It's risky. Too risky. And it costs money to launch a lifeboat. This boy's endangering us all with this wild goose chase.* But he needed to be there if Gloria was inside.

'Don't take your life-jacket off.' Frank's tone was gruff, but Saul was grateful for his kindness.

One after the other they clambered off the boat and onto the ladder. The fort was like a monster, rising from the deep.

The waves were so loud that Saul could no

longer hear Frank's voice. All he could hear was the clanging of a buoy's bell. It marked the edge of the shipping channel. Blackness surrounded them both. He felt exposed and clung to the metal rungs, the wind attacking them. But then it was over. They were climbing over the top of the ladder into the relative dryness of the fort.

It took Saul's eyes a few moments to adjust. Frank was carrying a torch and he shone it around the room. It was frozen in time. Decades of history.

The walls were intact, but peeling and rusty. A few hard-backed chairs were dotted about the place. An oil lamp rested on a scratched coffee table. On the floor was a rug stained with dirty water that had leaked from the roof.

And there, in the corner, was a woman's body.

At first, Saul was convinced she was dead. The woman was lying on her side, her back to them. There was blood in her hair. And the position of her body looked unnatural. Frank let out a cry and radioed his colleagues in the lifeboat below. Saul took a step towards her. He was unsure of how he felt about this broken heap of a person.

'Gloria,' he said. 'It's me.'

At the sound of his voice, Saul's mother turned painfully towards her son. Bruises marked her face. Her lips were swollen, as if she'd been beaten. She smiled and grimaced at the same time. 'I knew you'd come.'

Everything happened in a blur after that. The lifeboat volunteers helped lift his mother down the ladder and into the boat. Someone radioed ahead for an ambulance. Saul sat in the lifeboat and held his mother's hand.

'Who did this to you?' he said. But her eyes were closed and she didn't answer.

Frank patted Saul on the shoulder. 'You did a good job, champ.' And Saul allowed himself to feel a flicker of pride.

The lights of the shoreline were beacons of hope in the dark. Saul fixed his gaze on them, to remind himself that they were safe now. But anger burned inside him. The swell of the waves was dizzying. But his mind was crystal clear. Whoever had done this would live to regret it.

And then Southend Pier came into view. The bright colours of the amusement arcades and the fairground rides. The safety of the lifeboat station. A medical team was waiting for Gloria. And there, out of the darkness, stepped Etta Fitzroy, the detective who was no longer a detective.

18

Thursday

As soon as she'd seen the lifeboat cross the estuary, Etta realized her mistake. The rescue operation had been launched from further along the coast. Naturally, that's where it would return to. She called a taxi and was waiting on the quayside when the lifeboat docked.

Paramedics got to work on Gloria immediately. Etta was alarmed by her pale face and the extent of her injuries. As soon as she saw her, Saul's mother croaked out an apology. It was she who had let slip to her captors the former detective's name. 'Did they hurt you?' she said, her hands fluttering in distress. Etta thought about Nate's vandalized grave. There were more ways to inflict pain than physical.

But she shook her head. 'No, they didn't.' Then breathed out her relief. Gloria was in safe hands. She was going to survive. Etta's main concern now was Saul. 'You found her,' she said.

'Good detective work.' And for the first time, Saul had offered her that shy half-smile.

She took in the bruises around his eyes. The gaunt hollows of his face. 'Wait there,' she said. A few minutes later, she returned with a can of Coke and some doughnuts.

While he was eating, she asked one simple question. 'What happened to you?'

Saul bit his lip, as if battling with himself. Then he made a decision. He told her about the sea fort and the men who had threatened him. The registration plate he'd found on Gloria's phone. And Etta knew she'd been right to return. The pieces of the puzzle had been there. They'd just needed to fit them together in the right way.

The ambulance left for the hospital with Gloria inside. One of the lifeboat volunteers offered to take Saul and Etta. In the over-bright light of the hospital waiting room, Etta called Toni and The Boss. Within an hour, two officers from Essex Police had arrived to take their statements.

'Where are you going to stay tonight?'

Saul looked at her, surprised. 'The flat.'

'I'm not sure that's a good idea. Are you?'

'I'll be fine.'

'Do you want me to stop over? I can sleep on the sofa.' And for the second time, a look of surprise crossed his face. He refused her offer. Saul was not used to kindnesses.

'Take care of yourself,' said Etta when it was time to leave. 'In the nicest possible way, let's hope we don't meet again.'

And Saul had laughed then, and so had she.

An officer from Essex Police drove Etta back to the train station. On the spur of the moment, she'd brought forward her flight home and was due to leave for New York in a couple of days.

She replayed the earlier conversation she'd had with The Boss. 'Are you sure you won't come back? We need good detectives like you.' And she thought again of the boy with the white-blond hair.

She watched the estuary slide from view, barely visible in the night. She thought about how bone-tired she felt. And the magnetic connection that drew her to Saul. She wanted to help him because who else did he have?

And she was a mother without a son.

19

Monday

A few days later, two police officers knocked on the door of Saul's flat. He was on his way to the hospital to visit Gloria. The three of them stood awkwardly on the doorstep.

When it was clear Saul wasn't going to invite them in, the younger one cleared his throat. 'We wanted to give you an update.' He had a smattering of hair on his upper lip. He didn't look much older than Saul. 'That's right,' said the other one with a serious expression.

'What is it?'

'Do you remember the registration plate you gave us? The fish van?' The police officer didn't wait for him to reply. 'We traced the owner. He was a known drug dealer. He'd served time in prison for drugs offences. And it seems like he'd set up a lucrative business smuggling cocaine here in Leigh. He was using the nature reserve as a base.'

The younger man chimed in. 'We suspect he attacked you and kidnapped your mother to warn you both off. You messed up his supply lines by alerting the police.'

'What about the bodies?'

'It looks like they were his clients. He'd got himself into some kind of extreme financial difficulty. But he was careful. He was only picking off those who bought more than the average punter. The users who put in big orders and sold on to friends and acquaintances. He was taking their money, but keeping the drugs. He'd kill them once they'd paid him and dump their remains in the water. But the tide kept bringing them in.'

Saul gave a low whistle. He'd seen it for himself. The remains of the victims had ended up at the same spot on the island. The criminal must have banked on its seclusion. He'd assumed the bodies would never be traced back to him.

'And your father . . .' The younger one looked embarrassed. 'He may have been working for them, at some point. Probably had a falling-out. It's possible we'll never know.'

Saul feigned surprise. He knew how and why his father had died. But he wasn't about to tell them the truth.

The older one sighed. 'Anyway, the point is we

went to arrest him. But when we got there, it was too late.'

Saul arranged his features into a blank expression. 'Too late?'

'Yes, his house had been burned to the ground. With him inside it. The fire brigade found some empty bottles of vodka at the scene. There'll be an investigation, obviously. But they think the alcohol was used to speed up the spread of the fire.'

'I suppose that's what happens when you move in those kinds of circles,' said Saul. 'There's always someone out for revenge.'

Later that afternoon, Saul walked back alone from the hospital.

When Gloria had opened her eyes that first time after the rescue, they'd shone with gratitude. 'Thank you for saving me.' He'd sat by her bedside, her hand clasped in his. She'd told him how one of the men had bundled her into the van outside the pub. But she'd escaped and run to the flat. They'd caught up with her as she was trying to get her key in the lock. Kidnapped her. Left her to die in the sea fort. 'No one has ever looked after me like you do.'

But now she was feeling better, Gloria was back to her usual self.

'Can you buy me a bottle of vodka, Saul? Just one. I'll give you the money.' She'd used that wheedling voice he hated so much. When he'd refused, she'd called him every name under the sun. Some things never changed.

Back at their flat, he wandered into the kitchen. There were three leftover bottles of vodka under the sink. He smiled as he tipped them away. Remembered the taste of smoke in the back of his throat.

He gazed around the place he'd lived in for most of his life. The tattered furniture. The peeling paint. The smell of mould on a damp morning. In a few days, Gloria would be released from hospital. And his life would resume, the same as it ever was. He was stuck here. Trapped in an endless cycle. Why did he bother to stay?

The letter box clattered, making him jump. On the doormat was a package, addressed to him. He frowned. He wasn't expecting anything.

He carried it upstairs and placed it on the kitchen table. He could still smell the alcohol fumes in the air. With a sharp knife, he slit open the parcel tape. Some official-looking paperwork and a box tied up with a ribbon.

No one had sent him a present before. With trembling fingers, he undid the bow. He peered inside the tissue paper and his heart jumped in recognition. She must have taken it from New Scotland Yard. He couldn't believe she'd taken that risk for him. No one ever took a chance on Saul Anguish.

He slid the watch over his wrist and fastened the catch. It was heavy, weighted with memories of violence and pain. This watch had belonged to his father. It would serve as a reminder to Saul. While a part of Solomon's darkness lived on within his son, he would – could – never *be* him.

Saul turned his attention to the printed booklet. There was an image at the top of the page. A silver badge with a crown on top. In the centre of the badge were three notched swords, the county's coat of arms. It was an application form to join Essex Police.

A seed of hope took root. Perhaps Saul had a chance, after all. To flee this flat. To escape his mother and the future laid out for him. A Post-it note had been stuck to its front. *You'd make an excellent detective. I'll write you a reference, if you want. Think about it, Saul. It might just change your life. Love Etta.*

Acknowledgements

When I was little, my father would tell me bedtime stories every night. He couldn't read or write, but he didn't need to. Those stories came from a place deep within his imagination. Because he knew, even without access to the written word, that stories have power. To entertain. To inform. To make a connection between a father and his daughter long after she'd grown up.

When I was asked to be part of the Quick Reads campaign, my reply was a passionate 'yes'. My father left school at fourteen. As a boy, he was forced to stand in the corner and wear a dunce's cap. There was a sense of shame associated with not being able to read. At seventy-eight, it still lingers. It probably always will.

I love writing about Leigh-on-Sea, the place I spent my childhood and close to where I live today. In the interests of accuracy, the real-life Maunsell Forts are located about 9 miles from the end of Southend Pier. The ladders have been sawn off for safety reasons, but you can still visit them by boat.

As for the Chinese mitten crabs, it is true they have colonized an island – but it is at Chiswick Eyot on the Thames, not the nature reserve near Leigh.

Thank you to The Reading Agency for giving me an opportunity to write *A Boy Called Saul*, especially Emma House, Mike Gould and Hannah Boursnell. It's an honour and a privilege. Thank you, too, to my agent Sophie Lambert, commissioning editor Trisha Jackson, jacket designer Neil Lang, editorial manager Melissa Bond, copy-editor Amber Burlinson, publishing house Pan Macmillan – and to all the booksellers who support such a worthwhile scheme.

I wrote this book for Dad – and for every person who has ever struggled to read and write. The world of books is a thrilling one, filled with adventures of all kinds. This is where the journey begins. Everyone is welcome.

Fiona Cummins, October 2024

THE **READING** AGENCY | **Quick Reads**

About Quick Reads

"Reading is such an important building block for success"
— Jojo Moyes

Quick Reads are short books written
by bestselling authors.

Did you enjoy this Quick Read?

Tell us what you thought by
filling in our short survey.
Scan the **QR code** to go
directly to the survey or
visit: **bit.ly/QuickReads2025**

Thank you to Penguin Random House, Hachette and all our
publishing partners for their ongoing support.

Thank you to The Foyle Foundation for their support of
Quick Reads 2025.

A special thank you to Jojo Moyes for her generous donation
in 2020–2022 which helped to build the future of Quick Reads.

Quick Reads is delivered by The Reading Agency, a national
charity with a mission to empower people of all ages to read.

readingagency.org.uk   **@readingagency**   **#QuickReads**

The Reading Agency Ltd. Registered number: 3904882 (England & Wales)
Registered charity number: 1085443 (England & Wales)
Registered Office: 24 Bedford Row, London, WC1R 4EH
The Reading Agency is supported using public funding by
Arts Council England.

Supported using public funding by
**ARTS COUNCIL
ENGLAND**

Find your next Quick Read

In 2025, we have selected six
Quick Reads for you to enjoy.

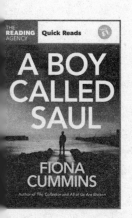

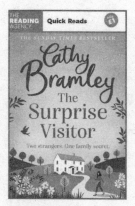

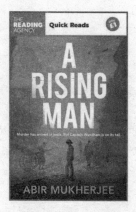

Quick Reads are available to buy in paperback or ebook and to borrow from your local library. For a complete list of titles and more information on the authors and their books visit: **readingagency.org.uk/quickreads**

Continue your reading journey with The Reading Agency:

Reading Ahead

Challenge yourself to complete six reads by taking part in **Reading Ahead** at your local library, college or workplace: **readingahead.org.uk**

Reading Groups for Everyone

Join **Reading Groups for Everyone** to find a reading group and discover new books: **readinggroups.org.uk**

World Book Night

Celebrate reading on **World Book Night** every year on 23 April: **worldbooknight.org.uk**

Summer Reading Challenge

Read with your family as part of the **Summer Reading Challenge: summerreadingchallenge.org.uk**

For more information on our work and the power of reading visit: **readingagency.org.uk**

More from Quick Reads

If you enjoyed the 2025 Quick Reads
please explore our 6 titles from 2024.

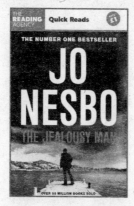

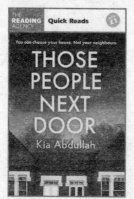

For a complete list of titles and more information
on the authors and their books visit:
readingagency.org.uk/quickreads

Discover more gripping and heart-pounding thrillers from

Fiona Cummins

'Complex. Inventive. Twisting. Unsettling'
Sarah Vaughan

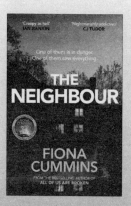

This Quick Reads edition first published 2025 by Pan Books
an imprint of Pan Macmillan
The Smithson, 6 Briset Street, London EC1M 5NR
EU representative: Macmillan Publishers Ireland Ltd, 1st Floor,
The Liffey Trust Centre, 117–126 Sheriff Street Upper,
Dublin 1, D01 YC43
Associated companies throughout the world
www.panmacmillan.com

ISBN 978-1-0350-6290-4

1 3 5 7 9 8 6 4 2

A CIP catalogue record for this book is available from the British Library.

Typeset by Palimpsest Book Production Ltd, Falkirk, Stirlingshire
Printed and bound by CPI Group (UK) Ltd, Croydon, CR0 4YY

MIX
Paper | Supporting
responsible forestry
FSC® C116313

Visit **www.panmacmillan.com** to read more about all our books
and to buy them. You will also find features, author interviews and
news of any author events, and you can sign up for e-newsletters
so that you're always first to hear about our new releases.